MR. MEN
and the Tooth Fairy

Roger Har

Original concept by
Roger Hargreaves

Written and illustrated by
Adam Hargreaves

EGMONT

Little Miss Curious was the sort of person who wanted to know everything.

She was the sort of person who asked impossible questions.

Questions like, "What does a tickle look like?"

Although, we know the answer to that one, don't we?

Little Miss Curious lived in a curious shaped cottage next door to an ordinary shaped cottage.

And in the ordinary shaped cottage there lived a little boy called George.

George and Little Miss Curious were good friends.

They sat out in the garden together under the apple tree and wondered about things.

They wondered about things like, "Why do trees have bark, but don't go woof?"

And things like, "Why do trees have trunks, but they don't have tusks?"

Not very long ago, the friends met under the apple tree and on this day George had something exciting to tell Little Miss Curious.

"Look!" he cried, grinning broadly. "I've lost my first tooth!"

"How strange," said Little Miss Curious. "I wonder why teeth fall out?"

"It's to make space for your big teeth to grow," George explained. "I'm going to put my tooth under my pillow tonight."

"Why are you going to do that?" asked Little Miss Curious.

"So that the Tooth Fairy will come and take my tooth and put a coin in its place," replied George.

"I wonder what the Tooth Fairy looks like?" asked Little Miss Curious.

George didn't know.

"I wonder where the Tooth Fairy lives?"

Again, George didn't know.

"What a lot of questions needing answers," said Little Miss Curious. "Now you have made me very curious."

After lunch Little Miss Curious met Mr Muddle.

"Hello, Mr Muddle," she said. "Do you know what the Tooth Fairy looks like?"

"Yellow feathers and a beak," replied Mr Muddle.

Little Miss Curious was sure that this was not the right answer.

Later that day she met Mr Wrong.

"Hello, Mr Wrong," she said. "I was wondering, do you know where the Tooth Fairy lives?"

"In a tree," replied Mr Wrong.

Little Miss Curious was sure this was not the right answer either.

So that night Little Miss Curious stayed awake and sometime after midnight when everybody else was sleeping, Little Miss Curious saw a soft green glow bobbing about outside George's window.

It was the Tooth Fairy.

"So that's what the Tooth Fairy looks like," Little Miss Curious said to herself.

She followed the Tooth Fairy to another house and this time she was able to peek through the window to see what happened next.

She watched as the Tooth Fairy took a coin from her purse, reached under a little boy's pillow and pulled out the tooth the sleeping boy had left there before he went to bed.

The more Little Miss Curious watched the fairy at her work the more curious she became.

Little Miss Curious followed the Tooth Fairy from house to house until the first light of morning.

She had to run to keep up.

As the sky began to lighten the Tooth Fairy flew away towards a wood.

And in the middle of the wood there was a clearing.

And in the middle of the clearing was a tree.

A very tall tree.

The Tooth Fairy flew up into the tree.

And of course Little Miss Curious, being the curious person she was, had to follow.

As the sun rose higher in the sky she climbed higher in the tree.

Higher and higher rose the sun, up and up went Little Miss Curious, until there in the top most branches of the tree she saw a miniature tree house.

Little Miss Curious peeked through the window and saw a little chair, a little table and a little bed.

And there was the little fairy herself brushing her beautiful teeth!

So now Little Miss Curious knew what the Tooth Fairy looked like and she knew where the Tooth Fairy lived.

Her curiosity was satisfied.

So she went home.

But on the way home she had a thought.

A puzzling thought that, not surprisingly, made her curious.

She went straight to Mr Wrong's house.

"You are clever. How did you know the Tooth Fairy lives in a tree?" she asked.

"Was I right?" exclaimed Mr Wrong. "How remarkable. I'm never right. Normally I am…"

"… left!"

Which left Little Miss Curious more curious than ever!